FOR LOVE
OF
FELICIA

Also by Alexandria Blaelock

SHORT STORY COLLECTIONS
The Histories of Hayward Hall
Lovelorn, Lovestruck and Love at First Sight
Common or Garden Variety Heroes
Case Files of the Wilkinson Detective Agency
Unavoidable Fates
Christmas Travesties
Five Faces of Felicia Clarke
Little Place Called Home
Security Directorate Dossiers v. 1.
Security Directorate Dossiers v. 2.

FICTION
That Love Nonsense
Taipan vs Brown
The Ghost and Ms Cox
Friends Like That
Weaving the Wildwood
Wolf vs Orb

MS BLAELOCK'S BOOKS
Stress Free Dinner Parties
Signature Wardrobe Planning
Holistic Personal Finance
Minimally Viable Housekeeping
Planning a Life Worth Living

PICTURE BOOKS
Australia Felix

SELECTED SHORT STORIES
Alma's Grace
Blood and Bloody Profanity
Cancelled by the Cartel
Dingo Hunting
Honoris Virilis Respectu
Mince Pie Mystery
Remains of Christmas

FOR LOVE OF OF FELICIA

A FELICIA CLARKE
SHORT STORY

ALEXANDRIA BLAELOCK

BlueMere Books
MELBOURNE, AUSTRALIA

For permission requests, please contact enquiries@bluemerebooks.com.

Ordering Information:
Discounts are available on quantity purchases. For details, contact orders@bluemerebooks.com.

For Love of Felicia/Alexandria Blaelock
paperback ISBN: 978-1-922744-06-7
digital ISBN: 978-1-922744-07-4

Book Layout © BookDesignTemplates.com
Cover Art © liqwer20.gmail.com via depositphotos

FOR LOVE OF FELICIA

Tom died relatively young.

Some would say too young; that he never really lived.

But by the end of his life, the way Tom looked at it, he'd met the love of all of his lives, and they'd done about as much as was possible, and he was satisfied with that.

Couldn't have asked for more.

Except that she'd married him of course, but other than that, nothing more.

Felicia was his first and only love, and he met her through a series of extraordinary circumstances at secretarial college.

He'd been working in a dead-end haulage job when his new employer took a chance on him, and his mathematical abilities.

Tom was so very grateful to leave his days of hefting boxes and bags on his back as he dodged nuggets of fresh horse shit and steaming rivulets of piss on the cobblestones.

So grateful he'd signed up to the college the very next day, vowing to make the best of it.

He did not miss the days when in his worn-out, newspaper padded boots missed their mark and landed squarely in the mess.

Nor did he miss the dust and ground-up manure getting in his eyes and ears, and smeared across his face and neck as he mopped up his dripping sweat with his filthy handkerchief.

Or staggering into a storeroom and trying to stack the goods more or less neatly before he collapsed underneath their weight.

Not in the slightest.

But he loved his new job, safe and sound and warm in the office. Even if he did have to stand all day at his desk, trying not to blot the account books with his leaky fountain pen.

The first chance he got; he was buying a new one. The best he could afford. Perhaps even something inlaid with celluloid.

And every day since, he thanked his dead parents for interceding. For getting him out of that mess and into a new, more respectable life and place of employment.

And into college where he met the one and only Felicia who changed the course of his life.

Felicia seemed like one of those ancient Greek goddesses; helpful, and very capable in an exotically no-nonsensically efficient way.

When she smiled her lopsided smile at him, revealing her one true flaw, he was a goner.

Fell good and hard, no holds barred, no returns in love with her.

Loved the way she tilted her head.

Loved the way a single tendril of brown hair broke free from her bun and curled lovingly around her neck.

Loved the bafflingly enigmatically crooked little finger of her left hand.

Fortunately, the class tutor arbitrarily grouped the class into pairs, and he was paired with her.

For ten whole weeks of evening classes.

And that meant, ten weeks of study groups and research trips outside of class hours.

It was a godsend.

At the time, he'd just moved out of the boarding house and was living alone in a tiny apartment in the city, quite near the college.

Naturally, she lived at home with her parents in the suburbs; a train ride away followed by a brisk twenty-minute walk.

However, they both worked in the City.

He made quick work of suggesting they met at the close of business in a small café near the college for a bite to eat before class.

Ostensibly to discuss their progress on their one assessable assignment.

But in reality, to charm her.

And conveniently, it seemed she didn't take much charming.

Not that she was anyone's, as evidenced by her swift and brutal rebuff of John Stone's advances.

But she was certainly amenable to his.

And he loved her even more for that.

That she dressed and acted modestly.

That she smelled of Ivory soap.

And her hand, when he first dared to touch it, was as soft as butter.

Not the rock hard in winter kind of butter, but the summer soft in the larder kind of butter.

After a while, she started to call at his apartment to collect him for their field trips.

The first time she arranged to call by, he walked home a foot above the ground.

But when he got home, and looked around his apartment, he promptly fell back to earth with a thump.

Panicked at the filthy, musty old place.

So he rolled up his sleeves and cleaned the place. Thoroughly with scalding hot water, carbolic soap, and elbow grease.

Then bought a table and a couple of chairs, a curtain to hang at the window, and a couple of new cups and saucers on the never-never so she didn't run screaming from the place.

And on the morning of the day she was due, a small bunch of fresh, cheerful daffodils to welcome her.

Then back out on the street to scavenge a plain, barely chipped pickle jar from the local trash to sit them in.

Felicia professed to be charmed by his digs and assured him she found them as neat, and clean as she had imagined.

Tom surreptitiously wiped his brow.

And made himself a promise that he would clean his apartment once a week, and tidy up every day before he left for work, just in case she called unexpectedly in the future.

Which of course she did.

The very next day as a matter of fact.

And every single one after that.

Blushing prettily, claiming to maybe have left something or other behind the previous day.

Tom wasn't fooled.

Though he was a little excited at her forwardness.

The first time he kissed her, was when he walked her to the train station after class.

On the bridge over the train line, in the days before you could enter from both sides.

The lamplight reflected from the low hanging clouds and glistened on the tracks as he leaned forward to pull her coat more closely around her neck to be sure she didn't catch a cold.

Suddenly, somehow, they were kissing.

Tom had no real idea what he was doing, but it seemed Felicia was in no way uncertain, as she wound her arms around his neck and pulled him closer to her.

He impudently put his arms beneath her open overcoat, linking them behind her back.

The kiss was magnificent.

He never wanted it to end.

But she had a train to catch - the last train of the day in fact, and he reluctantly let her go.

Though it wasn't much longer before he kind of, sort of, delayed her return so long she missed the train.

Not that she was upset about that.

Or even that she was forced to stay over at his place for the lack of having enough money to stay anywhere else.

Knowing she couldn't contact her parents and tell them not to worry.

He started to feel guilty.

But later that night, in his moonlit bedroom, as he peeled the clothes, one by one from her willing body, the feeling eased.

And as he revelled in her soft, creamy skin, the faded smell of lavender stuffed drawer sachets, and the warmth of her body, he forgot it altogether.

She must have suffered some kind of repercussion for her overnight absence, but she never breathed a word of it to him.

Just made sure that they didn't waste any time dawdling between class and his apartment, and making sure she made it to the station with plenty of time to spare for the last train.

And of course, as time passed, he asked her to marry him.

She was reluctant, as to do so would be the end of her career.

But, she hastened to add, her reluctance had nothing to do with him personally.

She loved him.

She wanted to be with him.

But for the moment at least, her career came first.

She hoped he understood.

And to be honest, he didn't.

But he didn't want to lose her either.

So, he was prepared to wait.

For as long as it took.

For her to want to marry him more than she wanted or needed her job.

Because in a roundabout way, through horse shit and piss, he did understand.

If losing his office job was bad, how much worse it must be for her.

Given how much more restricted the opportunities for respectable avenues of work for women outside the home were.

He recalled his mother, after his father died, struggling to find and keep work while taking care of him and his three younger sisters.

How he had given up on his dream of an office job for their sake and taken the first job that offered enough money to see them taken care of.

So, he accepted her terms, and they carried on as they had been.

Living as much as man and wife as she would allow, before putting her on the last train at the end of the day.

She counted the days so she didn't get pregnant, and ruin her life.

Their lives.

All was well for many years.

So well his colleagues and friends started teasing him about making an honest woman of her.

Surely he'd made enough money to set her up comfortably now?

He blushed and stuttered, and they roared with laughter.

He mentioned it once more to Felicia, but she said if anything, her circumstances were such that she was even more reluctant to marry him.

Her career had progressed, she had more responsibility and was making more money.

But her love for him was unchanged, and she hoped he understood.

This time, it felt a little personal.

However, he still loved her.

And if not marrying her was what it took to keep her, then he would not marry her.

Now, it so happened that one day at work, he was walking under the stairs when someone up above dropped an empty crate.

It fell, crashing from floor to floor, and by the time it reached the ground where Tom was walking, it was mostly kindling. Grazing his face as it landed on his shoulder when he didn't back away fast enough.

Yes, it hurt, but he gave his face a quick wash with his handkerchief, thanked his dead parents for keeping him safe, and got back to work.

A few days later, his jaw ached, but he didn't really think much of it.

Just put it down to a little stiffness from the falling crate incident.

But a few days more and his jaw was clenching, and his arms and shoulder were spasming.

He knew something was wrong, and just in case, he wrote an informal will, leaving everything to Felicia.

That afternoon, his back and neck were arching. And a little after that, he was having trouble breathing.

His boss panicked and called an ambulance.

The doctor at the hospital declared it was tetanus.

Which was in those days, a death sentence.

A relatively quick, but very painful death, with nothing available in the way of treatment.

Just a little pain management to keep him more or less comfortable.

Felicia was distraught.

Holding his hand, begging him to get better.

Promising to marry him if he didn't die.

He couldn't say anything in reply, only grin as his face spasmed, and groan as his body arched making his bones creak.

The nurses hustled the horrified Felicia away.

Within fourteen days of being stuck by the remains of the crate he was gone.

Knowing that at least he had provided her with a fully paid-up funeral and life insurances, his savings and bits and pieces of furniture.

Enough that she could, if she wanted to, take a house and live independently of her parents.

As for Felicia, she never once looked at another man.

Whenever she was faced with an important decision, she asked herself, what would Tom do, then acted accordingly.

Knowing life was short and unpredictable, she only ever drank French Champagne, and ate fresh strawberries with cream every summer.

And when the tetanus vaccine was released, she was first in line.

THE END

As a small token of my thanks for reading...

Please enjoy 10% off everything (excluding shipping)

at alexandriablaelock.com

with the code tom10.

Turn the page for some ideas where to use it,

Do you have what it takes to be a hero?

Whether that's running into a burning building, standing up for what you know is right, or saving the Princess it's going to take everything you've got and more besides.

In this genre-spanning collection of original stories, five women draw on resources they didn't know they had.

Join them, if you dare.

Home is where the heart is

You can struggle to find the place you call home. It's not a place, it's a feeling. You'll know it when you find it.

This collection of short stories explores our search for a place we can call home.

Short, sweet and relatable, these stories will make you homesick for places you've never been.

Welcome to Wilkinson's

I'm afraid Mr Hall's running a little late, can I get you a tea or coffee while you wait?

No?

What if I tell you about some of the recent cases we've been involved in?

Get comfortable and settle in for a wild ride.

you go girl!
The opposite
of winning
isn't losing,
it's quitting.
· Martha Rosette Lutz ·
Time for
a nice cup
of tea and
a sit down
Time for
a nice cup
of tea and
a biscuit
there's a book for that

Time for a nice cup of tea
and a sit down
BEWARE THE EMPTINESS GREMLINS

Australian author Alexandria Blaelock writes mostly fantasy and mystery.

She's appeared in the Stringybark Anthology *Crowd Surfing*, *Pulphouse Fiction Magazine*, and *Ellery Queen's Mystery Magazine*.

She's also written five self-help books applying business techniques to personal matters like getting dressed, tidying up, and feeding friends.

Discover more at alexandriablaelock.com.

www.ingramcontent.com/pod-product-compliance
Lightning Source LLC
Chambersburg PA
CBHW051830180726
48283CB00004BA/1379